Christmas
Story Book

NEW YORK

CONTENTS

Cover illustration by Francis Phillips

Copyright © Marshall Cavendish 1982, 1983, 1984
This edition © 1988 by Marshall Cavendish Limited

First published in USA 1988 by Exeter Books
Distributed by Bookthrift
Exeter is a trademark of Bookthrift Marketing, Inc.
Bookthrift is a registered trademark of Bookthrift Marketing, Inc.
New York, New York

ALL RIGHTS RESERVED

ISBN 0–7917–0221–9

Printed and bound in Spain

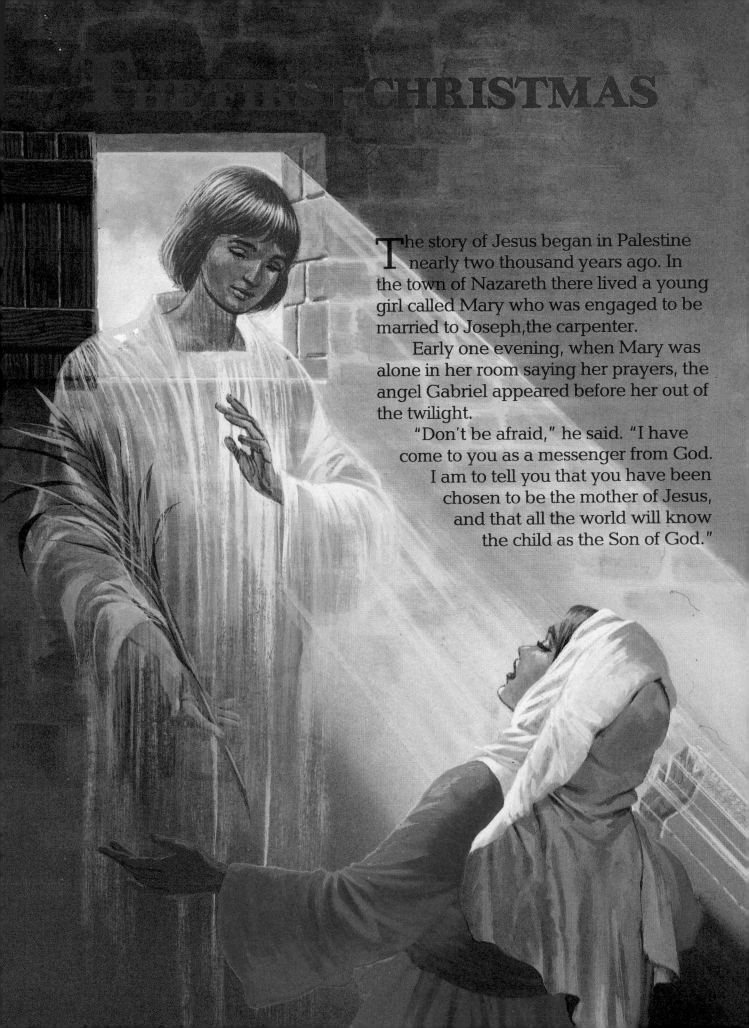

THE FIRST CHRISTMAS

The story of Jesus began in Palestine nearly two thousand years ago. In the town of Nazareth there lived a young girl called Mary who was engaged to be married to Joseph, the carpenter.

Early one evening, when Mary was alone in her room saying her prayers, the angel Gabriel appeared before her out of the twilight.

"Don't be afraid," he said. "I have come to you as a messenger from God. I am to tell you that you have been chosen to be the mother of Jesus, and that all the world will know the child as the Son of God."

Meanwhile, far away in Rome, the Emperor Caesar Augustus ordered that the whole of his great empire should be taxed. Everyone in Palestine had to return to the place their family came from, in order to be registered.

Joseph was of the family of King David, so he and his new wife Mary had to travel to Bethlehem, King David's ancient city. It was a long journey through dry and barren countryside. Mary rode on a donkey, and Joseph walked ahead to lead the way. Mile after mile they walked, and all the time the sun beat down on them.

At last they reached their journey's end. It was nightfall, and the town was thronged with people who had come to be registered. Joseph led the donkey through the narrow, crowded streets, searching for somewhere to rest for the night. But every inn and every lodging house was full.

Tired and hungry, Joseph and Mary were beginning to despair when a friendly innkeeper took pity on them. "I'm afraid I can't offer you a proper bed," he said. "There's no room at the inn. But you could spend the night in the stable. The roof is good and the straw is warm and dry."

Mary and Joseph thanked him for his kindness, and the innkeeper led the way to his stable.

In Chaldea, a country far from Palestine, were three wise and learned men who studied the stars as they moved across the heavens.

One evening, as the three wise men were looking towards the east, they noticed a star they had never seen before, and realising it heralded the birth of a great king decided to follow where it led.

The star lit the way towards Jerusalem. When at last they arrived, they went straight to King Herod's palace and asked to see him.

"Where is the child who is born to be Christ the King?" they asked. "We saw his star rise in the east and we have come to pay homage to him."

Herod was furious when he heard this news, but he hid his feelings from the three wise men. "What do the ancient prophets tell us?" he asked the chief priests.

"They say that Christ the King will be born in Bethlehem!"

Then Herod ordered the three wise men to go and search for the child. "When you have found him, report back to me," he said, "so that I may go and worship him."

The three wise men left Jerusalem and still the bright star guided them on their way. Sheltering from the heat by day, they travelled by night so as to follow where it led.

In the fields outside Bethlehem, some shepherds were minding their sheep. The night air was chill, and the sky was full of stars.

Suddenly a dazzling light shone down on them from the heavens, and a strange figure appeared.

"Don't be frightened," said the angel Gabriel. "I am God's messenger, and I have come to bring you joyful news for the whole world to share. Jesus, the Son of God, will be born tonight in the city of David. You will find the new born baby in a stable, lying in a manger."

And as the shepherds stood on the hillside, the whole sky was suddenly filled with light. Where there had been one angel, now there were thousands, all singing: "Glory be to God in heaven, and on earth peace and goodwill to all men."

At last the light faded, and the heavenly music came to an end. The shepherds stood in silence as the last notes lingered in the air.

Then one of them spoke. "Let us go to Bethlehem," he said, "to welcome Jesus, who is Christ the Lord." So they left their sheep in the fields and hurried down from the hills towards the town.

In Bethlehem, Mary lay down to sleep on the bed of straw that the innkeeper had made for her. Suddenly, she cried out and Joseph took her in his arms to comfort her.

all staring gently at the new born baby. Thus it was that the first people to pay their respects to the Son of God were not kings, or princes, or men of power, but simple shepherds.

After them came the three wise men, following their guiding star. When they saw Jesus they were overjoyed, because they knew that he was the king that the prophecies had foretold. Bowing low, they offered him kingly gifts of gold and frankincense and myrrh.

Mary and Joseph kept the baby safe until he grew into a young man. But, as the years passed, they never forgot the wondrous day Jesus was born — the very first Christmas Day.

"God's child is coming," she said.

And so it was that Mary gave birth to her son in the stable. She held him close while Joseph took his cloak and made blankets for the baby. Mary wrapped her son in the warm, woollen cloth and laid him in the manger.

When the shepherds arrived in Bethlehem, they found their way to the innkeeper's stable. In the dim light they saw the donkey, an ox and some cattle

We three Kings of Orient are,
Bearing gifts we traverse afar.
Field and fountain,
Moor and mountain,
Following yonder star.

O . . . Star of wonder! Star of night!
Star with royal beauty bright!
Westward leading,
Still proceeding,
Guide us to thy perfect light.

Born a king on Bethlehem plain,
Gold I bring to crown him again:
King for ever,
Ceasing never
Over us all to reign.

Frankincense to offer have I,
Incense owns a deity nigh;
Prayer and praising,
All men raising,
Worship him God on high.

Myrrh is mine; its bitter perfume
Breathes a life of gathering gloom;
Sorrowing, sighing,
Bleeding, dying,
Sealed in the stone-cold tomb.

O . . . Star of wonder! Star of night!
Star with royal beauty bright!
Westward leading,
Still proceeding,
Guide us to thy perfect light.

Glorious now, behold him arise,
King, and God, and sacrifice;
Heaven sings Alleluia:
Alleluia the earth replies.

O . . . Star of wonder! Star of night!
Star with royal beauty bright!
Westward leading,
Still proceeding,
Guide us to thy perfect light.

Christmas comes but once a year,
Or so the saying goes,
But many are the things to do
In the season of the snows.

Take a tray and find a slope
That's covered in thick snow,
Jump on your tray and all the day
Tobogganing you can go.

Pile the snow in great big lumps
By hand or trowel or spade.
With stones or coal for eyes and mouth,
A snowman you have made.

With your very warmest gloves,
Pick up some fresh clean snow,
And press it tight between your hands,
Then snowballs you can throw.

16

FUN ~

Being indoors on Christmas Eve
Is snug and warm and pleasant.
Hang up your longest, widest sock
For Santa's Christmas present.

With coal or logs upon the fire,
You need a fork for toasting.
Try crumpets, muffins, buns and bread,
And chestnuts slowly roasting.

When you've got your Christmas Tree
From garden, field or shop,
Put baubles, lights and tinsel on,
And a fairy on the top!

RUDOLPH TO THE RESCUE

Far away on the planet Gifto, Santa was having problems. There were many other planets to visit on his way to Earth, but Rudolph, his chief reindeer, was in bed with terrible toothache. And only Rudolph knew the way to Earth.

"We'll just have to rely on our computer," grumbled Santa, as he checked the instruments on his sleigh.
"Let's hope it works properly," muttered the other reindeer.

"Don't worry, Rudolph, we'll soon be back!" cried Santa, and he set off into space with all the reindeer except Rudolph. Poor Rudolph was near to tears. Santa's first stop was Three Moon Planet.

He found it easily, because there were signposts everywhere and not much traffic about. He made his delivery on time, and after a short stop for tea and sandwiches, he was soon on his way again. "Next stop Galacto!" he cried.

As the Milky Way flew by, Santa studied the computer. "That's funny," he muttered, "Galacto is supposed to be *here,* but there's nothing in sight."
The sleigh flew round and round for hours. At last, Santa and the reindeer bumped into a Space Police Patrol, who kindly offered to escort them to Galacto. "No wonder we couldn't find it," laughed Santa, "it's hidden behind this black hole!"

After delivering his presents to the children on Galacto, Santa was feeling quite pleased with himself. He was making good time and would soon be on his way to Earth.
Then suddenly, a meteor shower fell out of the sky and knocked the sleigh right off course. "Oh no!" moaned Santa, as the sleigh and the reindeer hurtled through space, "the computer's been smashed to bits! Now we're well and truly lost. I'd better call up Rudolph on my bleeper."

Rudolph was trying to get to sleep when the crackling message woke him with a start. "Santa needs my help . . . Oh! If only I didn't have this awful toothache."

Then Rudolph had an idea. He got some string, and tied one end to his tooth and the other to a shooting star which happened to be passing. TWAAANG! The tooth flew off into space. "Ooh, that's better," said Rudolph, and in next to no time he was speeding to the rescue. At last he spotted his friends, floating about among the stars. "Oh, Rudolph, I'm so glad to see you!"

cried Santa, and a great cheer went up from the other reindeer.
"Come on!" shouted Rudolph. "We'd better not be late for Earth!"
And sure enough, as night fell over Earth, little children everywhere peeped up into the sky and saw just what they wanted to see — Santa and his reindeer, racing over the chimney tops with a sleigh full of presents to deliver!

Away in a Manger

Away in a manger, no crib for a bed,
The little Lord Jesus laid down his sweet head,
The stars in the bright sky looked down where he lay,
The little Lord Jesus asleep in the hay.

The cattle are lowing, the baby awakes,
But little Lord Jesus no crying he makes.
I love thee, Lord Jesus! Look down from the sky,
And stay by my side until morning is nigh.

Be near me, Lord Jesus, I ask thee to stay
Close by me for ever, and love me, I pray.
Bless all the dear children in thy tender care,
And fit us for heaven, to live with thee there.

MORRIS'S CHRISTMAS STOCKING

It was Christmas Eve and Jane and the magic hamsters were very busy. Jane was making some of her delicious mince pies, Morris was decorating the Christmas Tree, and Doris was hanging up everyone's Christmas stockings by the fireplace. "I wonder what Father Christmas will bring us," she said.

"Father Christmas?" said Morris, as he tied the fairy to the top of the tree. "Surely you don't believe in him?"

"Of course we do," cried Doris. "Everyone knows it's Father Christmas who puts presents in our stockings."

On Christmas morning Morris and Doris and Jane rushed downstairs. All the stockings were bulging with presents — even Morris's. "See!" cried Doris. "Father Christmas *has* visited us!"

She opened her stocking and found some nuts, an orange, a woolly hat and a new tin of magic moonbeams for making hamster spells.

"Hurray!" said Jane. "I've got some jelly babies, an apple, some paints and a pair of stripy socks. Aren't they lovely? What have you got, Morris?"

Morris opened his stocking, but all he found inside were some old pieces of newspaper and a note. It said:

If you think I don't exist,
I'll cross you off my Christmas list.
Signed: Father Christmas.

"I think it's just Grandpa wizard playing a trick on me," said Morris. "I think *he* filled your Christmas stockings. I still don't believe in Father Christmas," and I never will."

Just then there was a terrific puff of smoke and stars flew all over the sitting room. It was Grandpa wizard! Instead of the purple robe he usually wears, he was wearing a red robe with white fur round the edges. He looked just like Father Christmas.

"Ha ha! I knew I was right!" cried Morris. "It's just Grandpa pretending to be Father Christmas. Come on, Grandpa, where's my stocking?"

"I don't know," said Grandpa. "But I've brought a visitor with me. Why don't you ask him?"

25

"Merry Christmas!" said a deep voice from the fireplace.

"Look! It really is Father Christmas!" cried Morris.

"But you don't believe in me," said Father Christmas.

"Oh, I do. I do now!" said Morris.

"Are you sure?"

"Oh yes," said Morris. "I promise."

"Here's your stocking then," said Father Christmas.

Morris looked inside and found a banana, a whistle, a new magic hat and a book of songs. "Thank you very much, Father Christmas," he whispered.

"You're very welcome," said Father Christmas. "Now, how about one of the songs from your song book?"

"Oh yes," said Morris. And he and Doris and Jane and Grandpa all stood round the Christmas Tree with Father Christmas, and they sang and sang until it was time for bed.

JINGLE BELLS

Jingle bells, jingle bells, jingle all the way,
Oh, what fun it is to ride in a one-horse open sleigh!
Jingle bells, jingle bells, jingle all the way,
Oh, what fun it is to ride in a one-horse open sleigh!

Dashing through the snow, in a one-horse open sleigh,
O'er the fields we go, laughing all the way,
Bells on bob-tail ring, making spirits bright,
What fun it is to ride and sing a sleighing song tonight!

LEROY LEARNS TO SKATE

It had been snowing all night on Magic Mountain and the Magic Garden was covered in thick white snow. Digby the robot gardener was checking to see if his flowers were all right. Digby's mischievous puppy, Spot, was being naughty doing somersaults in the flower-beds.

"Stop that, Spot!" said Digby.

"You what?" said Spot. "Here, catch this." And Spot hurled a big snowball at Digby.

Digby bent down to pick up some snow, and stopped to look at something.

"What is it?" said Spot.

"Footprints," said Digby.

"They don't look like footprints to me," said Spot.

Just then they saw Polly the plane high up in the sky. "Hello, dears," she called, and landed beside them with a bump, making the snow shoot everywhere. Her little friends the Tumbledownies were piled into the plane's seats.

"What are you looking at?" cried the Tumbledownies, climbing out.

"Footprints," said Spot. "But we don't know who they belong to."

"Oh, this sounds exciting, let's follow them," said Polly.

Soon they found themselves beside the fish pond.

"Oh look, it's Leroy the lion. Whatever is he wearing on his feet?"

"Hello," said Leroy. "Do you like my new ice skates? I was getting so good at

28

roller skating, I thought I'd try skating on ice as well."

"So that's what the funny footprints are," said Spot.

"Watch," said Leroy, "I'll show you

how they work." He put his feet on the frozen fish pond and took one huge step.

"Watch out!" called Digby, but it was too late. Leroy went skidding across the pond towards a pile of snow. Crash!

"Oh dear," said Polly. "Are you all right, Leroy?"

"Yes," said Leroy. "But I'm never going to learn to ice skate. I've been trying all morning."

"Why don't you pretend you're roller skating?" said Spot. "You never fall down on roller skates."

"Good idea," said Leroy.

He stepped out on to the ice again, and started to skate just as if he was on roller skates. "Come on," said Leroy, "try it, it's great."

Spot jumped on to the ice, and so did Digby and so did Polly and the Tumbledownies. But as soon as they touched the ice, they all fell down.

"Well, I'm going to start my engine," said Polly. Her propellers started to turn, but all they did was blow snow everywhere.

"Help!" shouted the Tumbledownies as the breeze from Polly's propellers blew them across the ice.

"Help!" shouted Digby. "My motor's freezing up!"

"Help!" shouted Spot. "My fur's falling out!"

And then they noticed a big snowman standing on the other side of the pond.

"Where did he come from?" said one of the Tumbledownies.

"It's me," said the snowman. "It's me, Leroy. Polly's propellers blew so much snow over me that I couldn't skate any more."

"Well you look very nice as a snowman," said Polly. "Come on Tumbledownies."

And they all joined hands and danced around Leroy the snowman.

DOTTY AND THE TEDDY BEARS

Dotty, the magic dragon, was feeling very excited because her three little nephews were coming to stay for Christmas. She had been busy in the kitchen all day making lots of delicious food — and messy pots and pans!

When Dotty had finished the washing-up, the water in the sink would not run away down the plug hole.

"Oh no," cried Dotty, "the sink's blocked." Then she had an idea. She opened her mouth and blew one of her special flames down the plug hole. It went through the waste-pipe, made a huge hole in the kitchen floor and shot right down to a cave deep in Magic Mountain.

Dotty peered down the hole into the cave. All she could see was a huge pile of teddy bears.

"Hello-o-o," called Dotty.

"What do you think you're doing?" an angry voice yelled back. It was an elf, covered in dust.

"Oh, I'm so sorry . . ." Dotty began, but then she saw another elf.

"Who are you?" he asked.

"Why, Dotty the dragon of course!" she cried. "Hold on, I'm coming down."

Dotty climbed down to the cave and looked around. There were piles of teddy bears everywhere, and a row of elves were busy making more.

"What is this place?" Dotty asked the elf who had been so cross.

"It's the Teddy Bear Division of Santa's Toy Workshops," he said. "We make all the teddy bears that Santa gives children at Christmas. But we still have hundreds to make before Santa comes to collect them — and we don't have enough pairs of hands."

"Hmm," said Dotty, "I think I can help you. I'll be back in two seconds."

Dotty whizzed up to her kitchen, got her magic dish-mop and whizzed back down to the cave. She waved her dish-mop at a pile of teddies. At once they jumped up and began making more and more teddies, just like themselves. The elves were amazed.

"Now, elves," said Dotty, "while the teddies are nice and busy down here, you must come to my house and have a rest."

"Ooh, thanks, Dotty," said the cross elf, who had stopped looking cross.

The elves went up to Dotty's kitchen, ate some mince pies and put their feet up. But as they were dozing in front of the television, they heard bangs and crashes from the cave below.

They rushed down to the cave to see what was happening.

There were teddies swinging from the lights, and teddies jumping off shelves, teddies chasing each other and teddies knocking each other about.

"You naughty teddies! Ah! Just look at the state you're in!" shrieked Dotty.

At once they all stopped what they were doing and looked down at

themselves. They were dusty and their bows were coming undone.

"Santa won't give you to any nice children looking like that," said Dotty. "Quick, clean yourselves up before he gets here."

The teddies helped make each other neat and tidy again, while the elves counted them.

"Goody," they said. "We've got enough teddies for Santa now."

"Well, I'll leave you all to it," said Dotty, and as she left she could see the elves winking at each other. She could not understand why — but when her three nephews looked in their stockings on Christmas morning, what do you think they found? Peeping out of the top of each one was a very cheeky-looking teddy bear, with its bow very neatly tied.

Clara and the Nutcracker Doll

It was Christmas Eve, and Clara and Franz were waiting for their godfather, Uncle Johann, to arrive. He came to visit them every year to give them their Christmas presents himself. They were very special presents, because Uncle Johann was a toymaker.

"Perhaps he'll come if we shut our eyes and think about him very hard," said Clara.

"Don't be silly," said Franz.

"Oh, let's just try," said Clara. So they both shut their eyes tight and thought very hard.

Just then the doorbell rang. "It worked!" cried Clara, and in came Uncle Johann laughing and shaking the snow off his coat.

"Well, well, well," he cried, hugging them both. "Here you are then. What do you think of these, my little friends?"

He gave Franz and Clara a parcel each. Inside Franz's was a beautiful wooden boat with a bright red sail, and inside Clara's was a doll with very long legs, painted to look like a soldier.

"Who is he?" asked Clara.

"He's a nutcracker doll," said Uncle Johann. "Look." He picked up a nut from a dish on the table, placed it in the doll's mouth, pulled the legs close together and hey presto! The nut's shell cracked open in two neat halves. Uncle Johann popped the nut into Clara's mouth. Clara was thrilled.

"Oh he's lovely, Uncle Johann. I've never had a nutcracker doll before."

And she danced round the room holding her new doll above her head. Her brother Franz had been watching her all this time, not saying a word. Suddenly, he dashed across the room, snatched the doll, threw it onto the floor and jumped on it. Clara burst into tears. "Oh no! My poor doll!"

Uncle Johann strode across the room, picked up Franz and bundled him out of the door. Clara could hear him speaking very angrily to Franz, as she picked up the nutcracker doll and looked closely at it. She began to smile through her tears. "So, you're not broken after all," she whispered. She curled up on the sofa, with the doll in her arms, and went to sleep.

Later that night, Clara woke to find herself tucked up in her own bed.

"They must have brought me upstairs when I was asleep," she thought. "But where's my nutcracker doll? He must have fallen on the floor again, poor thing."

Quiet as a mouse, Clara put on her slippers and crept downstairs. The clock struck midnight as she opened the door to the drawing room. Startled, she darted across the floor, leaped on to the sofa, and tucked her feet inside her nightdress. She looked all around her.

The fire flared in the grate and lit up the room. Just then there was the sound of stamping feet, and rows of mice came marching by, led by a mouse king with fierce, bright eyes.

Clara's own eyes grew wider and wider as columns of soldiers marched in from the other end of the room. They were Franz's toy soldiers, and leading them was her nutcracker doll!

The mice and the toy soldiers started to fight. In minutes, the mouse king had driven the nutcracker doll right up against the sofa where Clara was sitting. "Oh no you don't!" she thought.

In a flash, she had taken off a slipper and thrown it at the mouse king. Stunned, he fell to the floor. The nutcracker doll toppled over too and hit his head. The mice rushed forward and carried their king away to safety.

Clara started to pick up the nutcracker doll, but as she did so, quick as a flash, he grew and grew before her very eyes. He was no longer a doll, but a handsome young man. He picked up Clara's slipper, kissed it and gave it back to her.

"Oh yes, please. How do we get there?" Scarcely had she spoken when a boat appeared. Clara and the Prince stepped into it and skimmed off through the wintry night. Snowflakes whirled and danced around them, but Clara felt as warm as if she were wrapped in eiderdown.

At last they arrived at the Nutcracker Prince's palace. Clara gazed at it, entranced. It was made from white icing, with towers of pink icing, columns of barley sugar and chandeliers of glistening pear-drops.

A beautiful, dainty lady welcomed Clara as though she were a princess.

"I am the Sugar Plum Fairy," she said, "and I have all kinds of treats to show you."

"You saved my life. I shall not forget it," he said, smiling at her.

"Who *are* you?" stammered Clara.

"I am the Nutcracker Prince. Will you come with me to my kingdom? It is the Kingdom of Sweets, and no human being has ever visited it before."

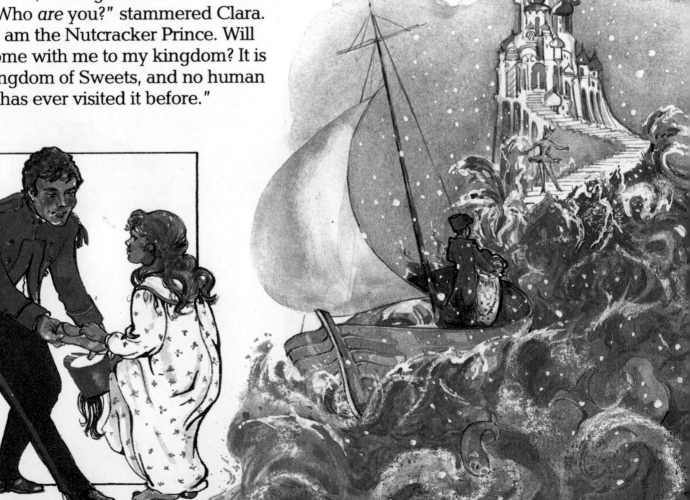

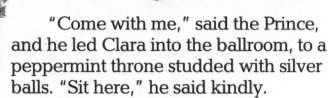

"Come with me," said the Prince, and he led Clara into the ballroom, to a peppermint throne studded with silver balls. "Sit here," he said kindly.

"But what is going to happen?"

"All your favourite sweets will dance for you," said the Prince. He smiled and put his finger to his lips as music filled the ballroom.

Clara's heart beat with excitement as two dancers leaped into the middle of the ballroom. They were dressed in rich brown velvet, and Clara watched enthralled as they weaved and stamped to and fro.

"They must be chocolates — my favourite!" she whispered to the Prince. And as if by magic, the dancers became chocolates.

Next came a dozen children, skipping and tripping in candy-coloured dresses.

"Fruit drops!" said Clara, clapping and laughing. "How I love them!"

Then two very tall thin men, dressed in black from head to foot, wobbled to and fro in front of her, in a most comical way.

"Oh, there's no mistaking them! They're Franz's favourite — liquorice!"

In another minute, the Prince had taken Clara's hand and led her on to the dance floor. They whirled around together so fast that the pear-drop chandeliers, the peppermint throne and the walls of white icing all mixed into one bright blur of light.

"Now for the loveliest surprise of all," said the Prince, as he led Clara back to the peppermint throne.

There was a dainty tinkling of music as the Sugar Plum Fairy stepped into the centre of the ballroom. She danced tirelessly, like a snow crystal floating on the wind, and Clara could not take her eyes off her for a second.

"Can she be real?" she wondered, and as she did so she looked down and saw that she was holding her nutcracker doll in her arms.

She blinked, sat up, and looked around. She was once more in her own bed, and the Prince, the ballroom and the Sugar Plum Fairy had all melted away.

"How very strange," thought Clara, and she snuggled down under the covers again, the nutcracker doll under her arm. "I wonder if I will ever see the Kingdom of Sweets again?"

And she fell fast asleep.

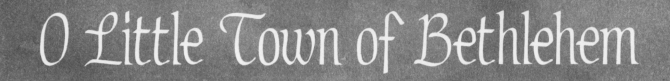

O Little Town of Bethlehem

O little town of Bethlehem,
How still we see thee lie!
Above thy deep and dreamless sleep
The silent stars go by.
Yet in thy dark streets shineth
The everlasting light;
The hopes and fears of all the years
Are met in thee tonight.

O morning stars, together
Proclaim the holy birth,
And praises sing to God the King,
And peace to men on earth;
For Christ is born of Mary;
And, gathered all above,
While mortals sleep, the angels keep
Their watch of wond'ring love.

THE FORGOTTEN TOYS

Koo the toy kangaroo sat on the pavement beside the big grey dustbin. "Boo hoo!" he sobbed into his glossy brown fur.

"Hello. Why are you crying?" said a friendly voice.

Koo looked up and saw a pretty rag doll peering at him through a mop of curly brown hair.

"Oh," he sniffed, "I was a little boy's best Christmas present, but he didn't like me. So I've been left out for the dustmen to take away. I wish I had a home."

"Don't worry," said the rag doll. "I was a little girl's best Christmas present, but she didn't like me when she found I didn't wet my nappy or say Mama. Now I haven't got a home either."

"What's your name?" said Koo.

"Ra-Ra," said the rag doll. "Shall we run away?"

"Yes, let's," said Koo. "We could travel a long way together and have great adventures. Kangaroos are great hoppers you know."

Ra-Ra jumped on to Koo's back and together they hop-hopped off down the road. It was late. Houses were locked up for the night and children were fast asleep in their beds.

"Isn't it cold?" said Koo.

"And quiet," said Ra-Ra. They both began to wish they were tucked up in bed like the children.

"Let's find somewhere to sleep," said Ra-Ra.

"OK," said Koo and he turned down a narrow alleyway. Hop, hop, hop.

Suddenly a big black shape landed — plop! — just in front of them. It was a cat.

"Hello," said the cat. "I don't often see people like you down my alley. I'm Sid. Who are you?"

"Sure," said Sid. "I'll be out all night, but I'll see you in the morning. Sleep tight." And he winked and ran off. Koo and Ra-Ra snuggled up and went to sleep.

"I'm Ra-Ra, the rag doll, and this is my friend Koo the kangaroo. We're Christmas presents nobody wanted."

"Yes," said Koo, looking sad. "We thought we'd go on an adventure — but really I would rather be a Christmas present that somebody does want."

"Can we stay here for the night, please?" said Ra-Ra.

Early next morning Sid woke them up. He was looking very pleased with himself. "Follow me," he said. "I've found just the place for you two."

Ra-Ra climbed on to Koo's back and they followed Sid along back streets and main streets until they came to a large building in a square.

"What a huge house," said Koo.

"It's not a house. It's a hospital," said Sid. "Wait here a minute." He winked and disappeared.

Soon the two toys heard footsteps.

They looked up and saw a woman in a blue dress and a white pinafore.

"Why," she said, "somebody has left us two lovely toys. How kind! The children will love them."

She bent down and picked up Koo and Ra-Ra and carried them into the hospital looking very pleased.

"Oh, look!" cried the children. "A toy kangaroo! And a rag doll! Aren't they lovely!"

Koo and Ra-Ra looked at each other happily. "Home at last," said Koo.

Minnie's Dinner Spell

Minnie the witch hummed as she flicked through her spell book.

> "Christmas is coming,
> I've got a good idea,
> I'm going to make my dinner
> By magic appear."

Then she stopped at page 394. "This is what I want," she said. "A spell to make a turkey."

She read the spell carefully.

> "Hens cluck and ducks quack,
> But Christmas turkeys gobble,
> And that is what I want to have,
> With a hubble bubble bobble!"

There was a bang and a flash and a loud gobble gobble! A huge turkey stood in front of her — a rather angry looking turkey. "Gobble gobble gobble!" it squawked, and lowered its beak threateningly at Minnie.

"Go away!" she shrieked. "Go away!

You're not what I wanted at all."

The turkey turned on its heel and waddled away, gobbling angrily.

"I meant it to be a cooked turkey," muttered Minnie, leafing through her spell book. "I'll try this spell.

> "One potato, two potato,
> Three potato, four,
> I want my Christmas dinner,
> To come flying through the door."

It certainly did! A large saucepan landed at Minnie's feet, missing her by inches. She jumped back in surprise.

48

"Goodness!" she said. "That spell worked." But when she opened the lid, she was disappointed.

"Mashed potatoes!" she cried. "That's not a Christmas dinner. Pah!" She slammed down the lid and picked up her spell book again.

"There must be a spell for Christmas dinner somewhere in here," she mumbled. "Ah, here's one that will do."

She cleared her throat and read,
  "Rice pudding, custard,
  Treacle and rum.
  I'd like a pudding
  Made out of plum.
  Alkafoozelum!"
Stars sparked and fireworks flared, and a round plum pudding with holly on the top appeared. There were even flames all around it.

"Hurray!" shouted Minnie. "I've done it! I've made my Christmas dinner!" And she danced a little jig.

But when she looked at the pudding again, the flames had grown higher and there was a strong smell of burning. Soon all that was left of the pudding were a few black cinders.

This time saucepans of mashed potato rained down on her. Big saucepans, little saucepans, saucepans with one handle, saucepans with two, black ones, green ones, even a gold one. And every one had mashed potato in it.

"Oh dear," moaned Minnie. "Something went wrong there. I'll just have to try a potato spell again. Maybe if I make it really strong, it will work.

"Ten potatoes doubled up,
That's ten and ten makes twenty.
I want my Christmas dinner,
And I want it to be plenty!"

Sadly, Minnie sat down. "I'll just have to eat mashed potato for my Christmas dinner," she sighed.

But then she had a surprise. The first saucepan of mashed potato tasted of roast turkey, the second of peas, the third of plum pudding and another of chocolate. Every saucepan of mashed potato tasted of something different.

"Mmmm," said Minnie, with her mouth full, "I don't know how I did it, but I've got my Christmas dinner after all. Now what does this potato taste of? Mince pies! Delicious!"

Mole's Winter Welcome

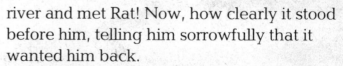

Mole and Rat were returning home across country after a long day's hunting with Otter.

They plodded along steadily and silently, Rat walking a little way ahead. So he did not notice when Mole stopped dead in his tracks, as though he had been given an electric shock. Mole's nose searched hither and thither — and again caught the smell that had so strongly moved him. And now he knew what it meant.

Home! His old home that he had hardly thought of since the day he first found the

river and met Rat! Now, how clearly it stood before him, telling him sorrowfully that it wanted him back.

"Ratty!" called Mole joyfully. "Come back! It's my home, my old home! I've just smelled it close by here, really quite close. And I *must* go to it. I must, I must!"

But Rat was too far away to hear Mole clearly. "Mole, we mustn't stop now, really!" Rat called back. "It's late, and the snow's coming on again, and I'm not sure of the way! Come on quick, there's a good fellow!" And he pressed on without waiting for a reply.

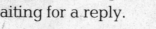

51

Poor Mole stood alone on the path, his heart torn asunder, and a big sob gathered somewhere low down inside him. But never for a moment did he dream of abandoning Rat. The smells from his old home pleaded and whispered, but he dared not stay any longer within their magic circle. So he followed in the track of the unsuspecting Rat.

After some time, Rat stopped and said kindly, "Look here, Mole, old chap, you seem dead tired. We'll sit down here for a minute."

Mole sank down forlornly on a tree stump, and the sob he had fought with so long rose up and up and forced its way out — and then another, and another, and others thick and fast, until he was crying freely and openly. Rat was astonished and dismayed at Mole's grief, and said very quietly and sympathetically, "What is it, old fellow? What's the matter?"

Eventually, Mole sobbed brokenly, "I know it's a shabby, dingy little place — not like your cosy quarters at River Bank — but

it *was* my own little home. And I went away
and forgot all about it. And then suddenly
I smelled it. And I *wanted* it! And when
you *wouldn't* turn back, Ratty — and I had
to leave it — I . . . I thought my heart would
break. Oh dear, oh dear!"

Rat said nothing, but patted Mole gently
on the shoulder, waiting for his sobs to die
down. Then he remarked carelessly, "Well
now, we'd better go and find that home of
yours, old fellow!" And he set off back the
way they had come.

"Oh come back, Ratty, do!" cried Mole,
hurrying after him. "It's too dark and the
snow's coming! And . . . I never meant to
let you know I was feeling that way about
it! And think of River Bank and your supper!"

"Hang River Bank, and supper too!"
said Rat. Taking Mole's arm he marched
him back to the part of the path where

his friend had scented signals from home.

Mole stood a moment, rigid, while his
uplifted nose felt the air. The signals were
coming through again! Like a sleep-walker,
he crossed a dry ditch, scrambled through a
hedge and nosed his way over a field.
Suddenly he dived down a tunnel, Rat still
following close behind. It seemed a long
time to Rat before the passage ended and he
could stand up and shake himself.

Mole struck a match, and by its light
they saw that they were standing in an open
space opposite Mole's little front door, with
'Mole End' painted over the bell-pull. Along
one side of the clearing was a skittle-alley, and
in the middle a small round pond containing
goldfish. From the centre of the pond rose a
fanciful creation topped by a large silvered
glass ball which reflected everything all
wrong, and had a very pleasing effect.

53

Mole's face beamed at the sight of these objects so dear to him, and he hurried Rat through the door of his home, lit a lamp and looked around. Dust lay thick on everything, and the neglected house looked altogether cheerless and deserted. Mole collapsed on a chair, his nose in his paws.

"Oh Ratty! Why did I bring you to this poor, cold little place when you might have been at River Bank by a blazing fire?"

But Rat took no notice. He was running here and there inspecting rooms and cupboards, lighting lamps and candles and sticking them up everywhere. "What an *excellent* little house this is! So compact! So well planned! We'll make a jolly night of it, you'll see! The first thing we want is a good fire. I'll see to that. You get a duster, Mole, and try and smarten things up a bit."

Mole roused himself and dusted and polished away heartily, while Rat soon had a cheerful blaze roaring in the fireplace. "Now come with me and let's see what we can find for supper." After hunting through every cupboard and drawer they found a tin of sardines, a box of ship's biscuits — nearly full — a sausage and four bottles of beer.

"There's a banquet for you!" observed Rat, as he arranged the table. "I know some animals who'd give their ears to be sitting down to supper with us tonight."

He had just got to work with the tin opener when they heard noises like the scuffling of small feet in the gravel outside, and a confused murmur of tiny voices. "Now, all in a line — hold the lantern up a bit, Tommy — no coughing after I say *one*, *two*, *three*."

"It must be the field-mice," said Mole.

"They go round carol-singing every year before Christmas, and they used to come to Mole End last of all for hot drinks and supper."

"Let's have a look at them!" cried Rat, jumping up and flinging open the door.

There stood about eight or ten mice, sniggering a little and sniffing and wiping their noses on their coat-sleeves. Then their shrill little voices rose up, singing one of the carols they had learned from their fathers.

When the singers had finished, they glanced shyly at each other, bashful but smiling. "Very well sung, boys!" cried Rat eagerly. "Now come along in by the fire all of you and have something hot."

"Yes, come along, field-mice," cried Mole. "This is quite like old times!" Then he suddenly plumped down on a seat, near to tears. "Oh Ratty, we've nothing to give them!"

"You leave all that to me. Here, you with the lantern, come here! Tell me, er, are there any shops open at this time of night?"

"Why, certainly, sir," replied the field-mouse respectfully. "At this time of year

our shops keep open till all sorts of hours."

"Then off you go at once, and, er, get me, er, now let me see . . ." Much muttered conversation followed and finally there was a chink of coins passing from paw to paw. The field-mouse hurried off with his lantern.

The rest of the field-mice all perched in a row on the bench and toasted their chilblains in front of the fire, while Mole made each of them recite the names of younger brothers and sisters who were as yet too young to go out carol-singing.

Rat, meanwhile, busied himself with brewing mulled ale, and soon every field-mouse was sipping and coughing and choking somewhat on the warming mixture. At last the field-mouse with the lantern appeared, staggering under the weight of a loaded basket. In a few minutes supper was ready, and Mole took the head of the table, watching his little friends' beaming faces. As they ate, the field-mice told him all the local news and answered the hundreds of questions asked.

Then, at last, they clattered off, showering Christmas wishes as they went, their pockets stuffed with treats for their little brothers and sisters at home. Then Rat said, with a tremendous yawn, "Mole old chap, I'm ready to drop. Is that your bunk on that side? Very well then, I'll take this. What a fine little house this is! Everything so handy!"

He clambered on to his bunk, rolled himself in the blankets and fell fast asleep.

The weary Mole soon had his head on his pillow, too. But before he closed his eyes he let them wander round his old room, resting on familiar and friendly things that glowed in the firelight.

He did not for a moment want to abandon his new life in the world outside, but it was good that he had come back to his own little home which had given him such a splendid Christmas welcome.

Santa's Sunny Christmas

Rudolph put his head on one side and scowled. "We never needed one before," he said doubtfully.

"We have to move with the times," said Santa as he tightened the last screw. His new parcelling machine was finished. "You see, the wrapping paper goes in here . . . the ribbon goes in here . . . and the present goes in this hopper and comes out at the back all wrapped and ready."

"Hmm," said Rudolph. "Very clever, I'm sure. I'll go and polish the sleigh."

On Christmas Eve, Santa was delighted that he had installed the parcelling machine. All the presents were wrapped. There was no last-minute rush. The sleigh was loaded, the reindeer were raring to go. Santa pulled on his boots and stood on the sideboard to check his suit in the mirror.

From the sideboard he could see down into the hopper of the parcelling machine. "That's funny!" Something was glittering in the bottom of the hopper. "What's that?" He looked down to try and see what it was.

"Ooh . . . aah . . . nearly . . . errh . . . ooow!" Santa toppled off the sideboard and into the hopper. The machine shook, whirred and swallowed him; wrapped, ribboned and parcelled him. Out came a neat, square packet at the other end.

"Santa? Time to go!" Rudolph put his head round the door. "Oh *now* where's he gone?"

The reindeer searched the house, the stables and the garden. They looked on the roof and under the sleigh. They looked behind the Northern Lights and under the polar ice-cap. But there was no sign of Santa.

Rudolph took charge. "This is an emergency, boys! It's already ten o'clock

and the whole world is waiting for Christmas. We'll have to make the deliveries ourselves!"

And that is what they did. They loaded the last parcels aboard — including the one they found in the parcelling machine — and set off across the snowy sky.

That year the noise was terrible in the chimneys. Stamping and grunting was heard on roofs. Sooty hoof-prints were found on fireside mats. But anyone who was woken by the noise kept their eyes shut and pretended to be asleep, for fear they got no presents.

Rudolph delivered each parcel to the address on the label. Sooty and sneezing, tired and tetchy, he was left with just one parcel on the sleigh. It had no label on it. "Just have to take pot luck!" he said, and hurled it off the sleigh.

The parcel spun dizzily down through the sky — missed the chimneys of Sydney, Australia, and landed — *splash!* — in the rollers off Bondi Beach. It rolled and tumbled in the surf.

A family of surfers came down to the beach to work up an appetite for Christmas breakfast. They spotted the box tumbling in the waves.

"Look! A free picnic! Cold turkey and cranberry sauce! Iced beer and Christmas cake!" They paddled out to the parcel on their surfboards.

But when they opened it, Santa poked his head out. "Oh! At last! Oh!" he spluttered. "Oh, phew, oh it's hot! What a relief! Thank you, thank . . ."

"Crikey, it's only a boring old Santa. No turkey! No beer! No cake!" and with angry hands they pushed Santa back into the box and tied the ribbons in a knot. The children were sad to see him disappear.

"He probably wants to go back to the North Pole," cried one.

"Yeah, let's take him round to the post office."

So they bundled him off to the post office and dumped him on the steps.

The postmen were exhausted after Christmas. They sat about on sacks of letters, yawning and rubbing their feet, but they were really rather sad that Christmas was over.

"Ah look at this, *another* parcel with no address on it," said the Postmaster-General when he found the package on the steps of the post office. "And late, too. Oh well, open it up, Bruce, and let's see if anyone wrote a name on the present inside."

So they opened it up, and out popped Santa saying, "Helpit'smelook-pleasedon'tputmebackinsideagain!"

The Postmaster-General was so astonished that he fell into a sack of letters and was almost posted to Walleroo.

In the corner of the post office were all the things that had fallen out of other parcels in the post: a jumped-on jelly, a crumbled cake, a squashed sack of sausage rolls. They did not look very nice, but they would still taste delicious!

"If we've got a Santa in the post office," cried the Postmaster-General, "we must have a Christmas party . . . well, a Day-After-Christmas party, anyway. Down to the beach!" And off they all went, taking their picnic in a mail-bag.

It just so happened that the glitter Santa had seen in the bottom of the parcelling machine was a kazoo. And the Postmaster-General was an amateur championship player of the kazoo. So he played, and the postmen danced on the sand, and so did Santa, and all in all everybody thought it was the best Day-After-Christmas party they had ever had.

"This is all very well," Santa thought, "but what kind of a Christmas is it when Santa and his reindeer aren't together?"

"What's the matter, mate?" enquired the Postmaster-General politely.

"Well, I'm having a wonderful time," said Santa, "but I must admit I do rather miss Rudolph and the other reindeer."

"Then send a telegram!" cried the Postmaster-General.

"Don't go, postman," said Rudolph grandly. "Gather round, all you other reindeer. We have been sent a telegram."

Opening the envelope, Rudolph read aloud,

ON BONDI BEACH. PLEASE COME. BRING BATHING COSTUME. LOVE SANTA.

Pausing only to find Santa's red and white bathing suit, the reindeer set course for Australia.

"Hello, reindeer! Ha ha!" said Santa jovially when they arrived. "Brought my swimming costume, have you?"

"It was behind your new parcelling machine," said Rudolph quietly.

"Well, if it weren't for that machine, none of us would be here," said Santa.

The postmen thought that the reindeer's sleigh would make a very good surfboard, and in no time Santa was skimming along the waves, crying joyfully, "Isn't Christmas lovely? Isn't Christmas *fun*?"

Back at the North Pole the reindeer were still searching frantically for Santa. "If we don't find him soon," said Rudolph, "I won't be able to stand the strain. Look at my fur. It's going grey with worry already."

Suddenly the doorbell rang.

"Telegram for you, Rudolph," said a small reindeer with a peaked cap.

Good King Wenceslas

It was midnight on Christmas Eve and Wenceslas was, as usual, very busy wrapping presents for everyone in the castle. There were silk stockings and silver skates for his dear Queen, a very difficult jigsaw for Albert, his page; pen-knives, nuts and marzipan for the footmen, and china ornaments and talcum powder for the cooks and under-cooks. And everyone had a tangerine each.

When he had finished, the King barely had enough time to tip-toe around the castle hanging a stocking at the end of each bed, before the whole castle was suddenly awake. So, as soon as Wenceslas had tumbled into bed, the Queen, page, footmen, cooks and under-cooks tore open their parcels, scattering string and paper everywhere, trying on stockings, munching marzipan and arranging ornaments.

What a to-do there was in the kitchen — a banging and chopping and scraping and basting; of spinach and roast potatoes, plum pudding, crème caramel and lime jelly, guinea-fowl, turkey and swordfish. Albert the page, having nothing much to do while the King slept, was busy tasting each dish and looking forward to his Christmas dinner. Meanwhile Wenceslas snored on and on. He was so exhausted with the night's work.

The Queen came in, kissed him, and gave him a pair of slippers embroidered with his initials. The King mumbled, "Charming my dear," and went back to sleep again. Albert, tiring of his hard work in the kitchen, came in and gave him a goldfish he had won at the summer fair. Wenceslas murmured, "Delightful, my boy," and went back to sleep again.

He slept on and on, while the Queen, the page, the Court and guests from far and wide ate their sumptuous Christmas dinner. Glasses were filled and refilled, crackers pulled and balloons popped. Then the court orchestra struck up and the entertainment started.

Six important guests from Italy performed a juggling act while standing in a human pyramid, the King of France rather unexpectedly danced the tango with his pet bear, and a Druid from Wales recited a long poem. This made everyone feel suddenly very weary, and the singing, laughter and shrieks of excitement died away. The whole party nodded quietly in their seats, the candles flickering low as the evening went on and. darkness fell outside, where silent snow had already fallen.

Wenceslas, meanwhile, woke up refreshed and full of energy. He stretched, jumped out of bed and pushed his feet into his new slippers. Walking over to his bedroom window, he leaned out, sniffing the frosty air with pleasure. Down below he spied an old man collecting firewood.

"I wonder who that can be, wandering about outside on a night like this?" thought Wenceslas, and he went to look for Albert, who with the Queen and all the guests was still snoozing peacefully in the dining-hall.

Wenceslas shook his page gently by the shoulder. "Wake up, my boy, I need your help," he whispered.

Albert rubbed his eyes, yawning and protesting. "Oh sire, I've eaten too much. I feel so-o-o sleepy."

"Come, my boy, we've got work to do. But first tell me — do you know who that old man might be I've just seen collecting firewood outside the castle?"

"Oh yes, sire, that's an old man who lives miles away at the bottom of the mountain.

He often comes over here collecting firewood."

"Hmm. Well now, fetch me as many pine logs as you can carry." Albert disappeared and Wenceslas went round the table, filling a basket with chunks of meat and decanters of wine.

When the page returned, staggering under a pile of logs, Wenceslas said, "Now, put on your warmest cloak. We're off to visit our friend at the bottom of the mountain and give him a surprise."

"But, sire, it's *freezing* outside!"

Wenceslas silenced him with a mild frown. "Just remember, not everyone has had the splendid Christmas that *you* have, or has a warm castle to live in."

And off they tramped in the snow. Wenceslas carried the logs, and Albert followed behind with the basket of food. They put it all down at the old man's door. "There," said Wenceslas. "Now at least he'll have a bit of Christmas dinner, and enough wood to last a few days."

Then they retraced their footsteps to the castle, Albert still following behind. As he walked, he felt the strangest thing — he did not know if it was because of all the food and wine he had had, but as he followed in his master's footsteps, his body tingled all over with warmth as though it was the finest summer's day.

"I wonder if anyone would believe me if I told them. No, they'd probably laugh at me. I think I'll just keep it to myself." And Albert snuggled up contentedly inside his cloak as the lights of the castle came into view.

Good King Wenceslas looked out,
On the Feast of Stephen,
When the snow lay round about,
Deep and crisp and even;
Brightly shone the moon that night,
Though the frost was cruel,
When a poor man came in sight,
Gathering winter fuel.

"Hither, page, and stand by me,
If thou know'st it, telling,
Yonder peasant, who is he?
Where and what his dwelling?"
"Sire, he lives a good league hence,
Underneath the mountain,
Right against the forest fence,
By Saint Agnes' fountain."

"Bring me flesh, and bring me wine,
Bring me pine logs hither;
Thou and I will see him dine,
When we bear them thither."
Page and monarch forth they went,
Forth they went together
Through the rude wind's wild lament
And the bitter weather.

"Sire, the night is darker now,
And the wind blows stronger;
Fails my heart, I know not how,
I can go no longer."
"Mark my footsteps, good my page,
Tread thou in them boldly;
Thou shalt find the winter's rage
Freeze thy blood less coldly."

In his master's steps he trod,
Where the snow lay dinted;
Heat was in the very sod
Which the saint had printed.
Therefore, Christian men, be sure
Wealth or rank possessing,
Ye who now will bless the poor
Shall yourselves find blessing.

DECK THE HALLS

Deck the halls with boughs of holly,
Fa la la la la la la la la.
'Tis the season to be jolly,
Fa la la la la la la la la.
Don we now our gay apparel,
Fa la la la la la la la la.
Troll the ancient Yuletide carol,
Fa la la la la la la la la.

See the blazing Yule before us,
Fa la la la la la la la la.
Strike the harp and join the chorus,
Fa la la la la la la la la.
Follow me in merry measure,
Fa la la la la la la la la.
While I tell of Yuletide treasure,
Fa la la la la la la la la.

Fast away the old year passes,
Fa la la la la la la la la.
Hail the new ye lads and lasses,
Fa la la la la la la la la.
Sing we joyous all together,
Fa la la la la la la la la.
Heedless of the wind and weather,
Fa la la la la la la la la.

I SAW THREE SHIPS COME SAILING BY

I saw three ships come sailing by,
    Sailing by, sailing by,
I saw three ships come sailing by,
    On Christmas Day in the morning.

Three pretty girls were in them then,
    In them then, in them then,
Three pretty girls were in them then,
    On Christmas Day in the morning.

And one could whistle, and one could sing,
    And one could play on the violin,
Such joy there was at my wedding
    On Christmas Day in the morning.

THE TALE OF THE LITTLE PINE TREE

It was the week before Christmas, and the forest of pine trees was covered in a crisp, white blanket of snow.

Morinda, a proud young pine, peered up at the older trees towering over her. "One day, I'll be as tall as them!" she thought.

Suddenly the silence was shattered by a high-pitched buzzing, and an agonising creak. A voice boomed, "Timber!"

A pine tree crashed down in the snow. "Oh no!" said Morinda. "It's those terrible lumberjacks with their chainsaws."

All day the awful din filled the forest. "I'm too young to be chopped up," muttered Morinda, watching the big trees fall.

But the young trees were being chopped down too, and poor Morinda felt the chainsaw tearing into her trunk.

The noise was deafening. Her branches shuddered and shook, and in a second she was tumbling down in the snow.

The young trees were loaded into a truck. "Now I'll become toothpicks," wailed Morinda bitterly, "or worse — *matchsticks!*"

That night the trees were delivered to the market. "Jingle Bells, jingle bells," sang Morinda, "we're to be Christmas Trees!"

Next morning Morinda fluffed out her branches and stood proud and tall. She was the most beautiful tree there.

People queued at Mr Spruce's stall to buy Morinda. But she was not for sale. Mr Spruce used her to attract his customers.

Soon all the trees were sold, and on Christmas Eve Mr Spruce took Morinda home for his family. She felt very special.

The Spruce children were very excited to see Morinda, and decorated her with baubles and tinsel. On her top they hung a star, and strung fairy lights all over her. "What a lovely tree!" they exclaimed. "Christmas *is* a happy time," said Morinda.

The Spruces' friends came to sing carols. "Let's sing in front of our beautiful tree," said Mrs Spruce. Morinda felt proud.

That night, when everyone was asleep, Santa Claus crept down the chimney. "Ho-ho-ho, best tree I've seen in years."

On Christmas Day, the Spruces opened their gifts and had dinner. Mr Spruce made a toast: "To the best Christmas tree ever!"

But, as the days went by, Morinda felt exhausted. "Oh no! My leaves are falling and my branches are sagging . . ."

On the twelfth day after Christmas, Morinda was stripped of her decorations and dumped on the rubbish pile.

She felt very depressed. "My life is finished," she sobbed. "Worms will eat me or I'll get wet and soggy and rot."

But Henri the sculptor spotted Morinda. "Oh ho ho! What a magnificent piece of pine!" he exclaimed and took her home.

He sawed off her branches, and for months he carved and chiselled her trunk. "What's to become of me now?" she sobbed.

At the Art Gallery, Henri unveiled his sculpture. Cries of "Oh magnificent!" and "Beautiful!" went up from the crowd.

Morinda glowed with pride, "I've become a famous work of art. Now I'll never be thrown away again!"

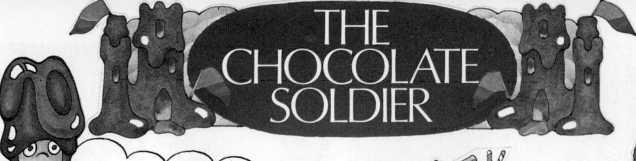

THE CHOCOLATE SOLDIER

Hector the chocolate soldier was very unlucky.

He lived in constant fear of melting. At picnics he could never sit in the sun.

He had to sit squashed under ladies' large hats —

or in the shade of trees.

He could never join the other toys at Christmas as they sat around the fire.

The fear of melting away was bad enough, but there was an even greater danger . . .

. . . and that was 'ORRIBLE OLIVER!
'Orrible Oliver was fat and lazy.

He loved eating all kinds of chocolate —
like chocolate eggs . . .

. . . and chocolate bunnies. But best of all,

he loved eating chocolate soldiers.

"I have to spend most of the day hiding
from 'Orrible Oliver," sighed Hector

to his friends, Edwina the Edwardian
doll and Pogo Woodenlegs.

With the help of Edwina
and Pogo, Hector always
managed to escape.

He wanted to
join his battalion in the land of snow,
where chocolate soldiers never melt.

"I'm going tonight," he whispered to
Edwina and Pogo Woodenlegs. "I'm
going to escape tonight!"

His friends said they would go with him.
So, at midnight, they all crept past
'Orrible Oliver's door.

They slid down the bannister and
through the cat door, and were soon
well clear of the house.

Then Edwina, the cleverest of the three,
said, "We must find the sugar mice.
They know the way to the land of snow."

They found the sugar mice on a stall in the fairground. "We're awfully fed up with being hoop-la prizes," they said.

"Can you help Hector find his battalion in the land of snow?" "Certainly! Climb on our backs!

"We'll fly you there — but watch out for the wicked snow giants!"

Suddenly a big snowball hit Hector and knocked him off his mouse's back.

"It's the snow giants!" More snowballs hit Edwina and Pogo Woodenlegs.

The friends lay in a crumpled heap. Slowly, the snow giants moved in . . .

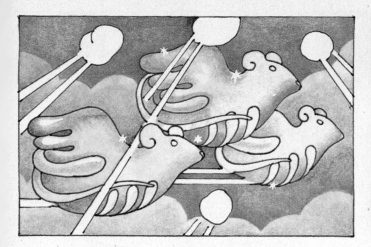

But the sugar mice flew on, through volley after volley of snowballs, to fetch help.

"Halt! Who goes there?"
"Quick! Quick! A chocolate soldier is in danger. So are Edwina and Pogo!"

"To the rescue! Sound the bugle!" The battalion moved out . . .

They arrived just in time, and when the snow giants saw them coming, they fled.

So Hector was back with his battalion in the land where soldiers never melt.

And when his friends said they would visit him, his happiness was complete.

TIMBERTWIG'S Christmas Tree

"Hello, Granny. Can I go out to play in the snow?"

"Of course you can. Look, I'm going out to find a nice Christmas tree for the front room. Why don't you pop over to see Mr Misfit and buy the decorations for it?"

Timbertwig did not need to be asked twice. He grabbed his coat and scarf and ran excitedly through Wiggly Wood. He had a marvellous time scuffing through the snow, sliding down the hills and even stopping for a quick snowball fight with the Tickling Trees.

Early one cold winter's morning Timbertwig woke up to find Wiggly Wood magically transformed by a blanket of sparkling white snow.

"Look Abigail!" he called as he picked up his hat. "It's been snowing!" Abigail the magic spider appeared at her little door wrapped in a rug and clutching a tiny hot-water bottle.

"D-d-don't I know," she shivered, her eight knees knocking together. "Your hat's like a fridge."

Timbertwig ran downstairs to find Granny Knot mixing the Christmas pudding in a large bowl.

"Now let me see," she mumbled. "A drop of beetleroot, a sprinkling of worms, and . . . oh, hello Timbertwig."

Eventually he reached Mr Misfit's Caravan of Surprises, settled in the corner of a snow-covered field. The rest of the travelling market had closed for the winter, but it was business as usual for Mr Misfit. Timbertwig entered the caravan and found him toasting muffins by his open stove.

"Come in Timbertwig, come in," he announced. "And what can I do for you?"

"Please Mr Misfit, I'd like your best set of Christmas decorations for our new tree," said Timbertwig.

Mr Misfit climbed up a rickety old ladder and found, squashed between the gas-powered bicycle pump and the turnip clock, a large cardboard box full of tinsel, fairy lights and brightly coloured glass balls. Timbertwig's eyes lit up when he saw them all.

"Aah! How much do I owe you?"

"Och, no, they're a present from me to you," smiled Mr Misfit. "And you can give your wicked old Granny a wee Christmas kiss from me as well!"

Abigail looked out from her door. "Well, we'd better hurry home. You do the running and I'll leaf through my book of magic spells."

When they got back, Timbertwig found the Christmas tree standing in a bucket, with a note attached to a branch which read:

"Dear Timbertwig, I've just popped out to collect some firewood. I hope you can have the tree decorated by the time I get back. Love Granny."

Timbertwig sank into a chair and sighed.

"Don't despair," announced Abigail. "I've just found the spell!" And she produced her magic stick.

"Wippity woppity zippity zee, Let decorations fill the tree."

There was a terrific bang and a magnificent blue flash — but not a decoration in sight.

Timbertwig thanked Mr Misfit and began to run home. He decided it would be quicker to go via Bilberry Brook, as the water would be frozen. Unfortunately, Timbertwig had never tried running on ice, and as soon as his feet touched the slippery surface his legs slid two different ways, sending the box of decorations crashing to the ground.

"Oh, no! What can we do? Everything is broken!"

"Oh Timbertwig, I'm so sorry," said Abigail. "I thought just for once my spell would work out all right, especially as it's Christmas."

Just then Granny Knot came running into the kitchen, her face beaming. "Oh, what a marvellous surprise!" she cried, wiping an icicle from the end of her nose. "When I said decorate the tree, I didn't mean you to go to all this trouble."

Timbertwig was confused at first, but when he stepped outside he soon discovered what had happened. The whole of the tree house was covered, from top to roots, with sparkling decorations.

"Oh Abigail, it *did* work," he laughed, hugging the little spider. "It really did!"

Just then Mr Misfit appeared, carrying a large hamper. "Oh, what a splendid job you've done there, laddie," he said.

"Ooh! what's in the hamper?" asked Timbertwig as they entered the kitchen.

"Och, it's just a wee Christmas dinner. I couldn't stand to eat it alone." And they all sat down to the best Christmas feast they had ever had.

A Christmas Carol

Jacob Marley was dead. As dead as a doornail. Nobody was very sad about it — not even his business partner, Ebenezer Scrooge. The only thing that upset Scrooge was the cost of the funeral.

Oh, he was a tight-fisted, grasping, scraping, clutching old sinner, was Scrooge! The cold meanness inside him made his eyes red and his thin lips blue. Nobody ever stopped him in the street to say, "My dear Scrooge, how are you? When will you come to see me?" But Scrooge did not care. He sat in his counting house all day long and counted money. "Ah ha!" he would say. "It's all mine, now that Marley's dead!"

That was where he sat one cold Christmas Eve. His clerk, Bob Cratchit — a thin man wrapped up in a long, threadbare scarf — was perched on a high stool. Just one lump of coal burned in the grate.

There was a rap at the window, and a chirpy young voice sang:

"*God rest ye merry gentlemen,*
Let nothing you dis . . ."

"Push off!" bellowed Scrooge, so ferociously that the carol singers fled down the road.

Bob Cratchit sighed. "Ah! Christmas! God bless it!"

"One more word from you, Bob Cratchit, and you'll lose your job!" snapped Scrooge. "Christmas? Bah! Humbug! I suppose you expect a whole day off tomorrow?"

"If it's convenient, sir," said Bob, rubbing his frozen hands together.

"It is *not* convenient. Why should I pay you a day's wages for no work? Eh? Christmas! Bah! Humbug! Humbug, I say!"

Old Scrooge locked up his office. Bob Cratchit ran all the way home to his wife and children. But Scrooge walked back to the cold dark rooms where he lived all alone.

By the light of a candle, he searched the rooms for robbers — nobody under the table, or under the sofa, or under the bed, or in the wardrobe, or in his dressing gown, where it hung on the door. He put on the dressing gown, his slippers and nightcap, and sat by the meagre fire to eat his bowl of gruel.

As he ate, the bell-pull beside his chair began to swing. The bell rang — softly at first, then louder. Soon every bell in the house was ringing. Scrooge dropped his spoon.

Just as suddenly, the bells stopped. There was a new sound — a clanking noise, as if someone was dragging a heavy chain. That someone was coming up the stairs — straight towards his door. On through the door it came, into the room.

and it's still growing!" Scrooge gazed at the ghost in horror. "I came to warn you, Ebenezer. You are to be haunted — haunted by three spirits."

Scrooge tried to say "*Humbug!*" but he could not. The ghost walked backwards through the window, and floated out into the bleak, black night. Scrooge went straight to bed, and tossed and turned until he fell asleep.

The clock woke him. It chimed a dull, deep, hollow, unhappy *one!* Lights flashed on in the room, and the curtains round his bed were drawn back. Scrooge sat bolt upright — and came face to face with a ghost!

"I am the Ghost of Christmas Past," droned the figure. "*Your* past, Ebenezer Scrooge. Rise and walk with me." The ghost took Scrooge's hand. Together they passed through the bedroom wall — and stood at once in a village street.

"Good heavens!" cried Scrooge.
"I know this place!
I lived here as a boy!"
A crowd of happy
boys were playing in
the snow and calling out,
"Merry Christmas!"

It was Jacob Marley!

His body was quite transparent. The clanking chain wound round him was made up of cash boxes, steel purses, keys and padlocks. "How now, Ebenezer!"

Scrooge felt deathly cold. "What do you want with me, Jacob? Why . . . why are you chained?"

Marley's ghost raised a frightful cry and shook its chain. "I wear the chain I made for myself during my life. These are the things I cared about — money, money and more money. Oh, Ebenezer, if you could see the chain that awaits you! It was as long as this one seven years ago,

But when Scrooge peeped in through the window of the school, one little boy was sitting all alone, reading a book.

"Nobody likes him," said the Ghost. "Nobody wants to play with him. All he wants to do in life is make a fortune."

"That small boy is me!" said Scrooge tearfully. "Me, when I was nine years old."

Suddenly they were no longer in the village, but inside a small, poor cottage.

"I've been here before, too!" cried Scrooge. "That girl on the sofa — oh, oh Ghost! Do you see how pretty she is? I was going to marry her once. Her name is Clara."

The young lady could see neither Scrooge nor the Ghost. Through her tears, she was trying to write a letter. Scrooge peered over her shoulder.

"*. . . You see, there is something you love more than me — money. So, my dear Ebenezer, I hope you will remember me when you are rich. Goodbye. Your own sweetheart, Clara.*"

"Take me home, Ghost!" cried Scrooge. "I can't bear it! I can't change what's past!" No sooner were the words spoken than Scrooge found himself in his own bedroom again. And where the Ghost had stood, a single candle flickered.

Scrooge was exhausted. It took all his strength to snuff out the candle before he reeled into bed and slept.

Waking in the middle of a snore, Scrooge *again* heard the clock strike one. There was a light coming under the door and a voice called, "Come in! Come in, Scrooge!"

In the next room, Scrooge found the jolliest of ghosts, dressed in a green robe trimmed with fur and with a holly crown on his head. "I am the Spirit of Christmas Present. Touch my coat!"

The walls of the room, and the night beyond it, melted away — and they stood in the snowy streets on Christmas morning. All the church bells were ringing, and people in their best clothes streamed out of the houses, greeting each other, and calling "Merry Christmas!"

The Ghost took Scrooge to Bob Cratchit's house where Christmas dinner was cooking. There was a dish of potatoes and a very small, skinny goose. When Bob arrived home, he was carrying his son, Tiny Tim, on his shoulders.

"Oh, oh Ghost!" whispered Scrooge. "The little lad is crippled!"

"The family is very poor," replied the Ghost. "If Tim doesn't get enough to eat he will die, and Bob's heart will break."

But nobody in the Cratchit family complained about the size of the dinner. Bob raised his glass to drink a toast. "To Ebenezer Scrooge, who pays my wages and so provided this meal!"

"God bless him!" cried Tiny Tim.

But Mrs Cratchit put down her glass. "Huh! Scrooge, indeed! I won't drink the health of that hard, cold, stingy man!"

Scrooge's face dropped, and he turned to the Spirit. "Take me home," he pleaded. "Please take me home."

But the Ghost had disappeared.

Somewhere a clock was striking one, and Scrooge saw a hooded phantom moving like a mist along the ground towards him. Its black cloak hid everything but one outstretched, pointing hand.

"You are the Spirit of Christmas Yet-to-Come," said Scrooge. "I fear you!"

It gave no reply, but pointed out some men Scrooge knew. They were laughing and talking. "When did he die?" said one.

"Never thought he would," said another.

"What's he done with his money?" asked a third.

"Don't know. But it'll be a very *cheap* funeral, because nobody wants to go! Ha ha ha!"

Scrooge tugged at the phantom's black sleeve. "Who are they talking about? It's terrible to talk of a dead man like this!"

Instead of answering, the Ghost pointed to the churchyard, and Scrooge crept, trembling, towards a newly filled grave. The cheap headstone had only two words on it:

EBENEZER SCROOGE.

"Oh Ghost! Oh! oh no, no!" He clutched at the phantom. "I'll be different! I will, I will, I *will*!" He clutched at that one, dreadful, pointing hand — clutched and held on to it, although it was hard and cold and as wooden as . . . as a bedpost.

Scrooge woke up clutching the wooden corner-post of his bed. The bedpost was real. The room was his own. And best of all, he was not dead!

"Oh! I don't know what to do first!" said Scrooge to himself, laughing and crying at once. "I-I don't even know what day it is!" Running to the window, he opened it and called to a boy below, "What, what day is it?"

"Why, it's Christmas Day, of course!"

"Christmas Day! So I haven't missed it!" crowed Scrooge. "Hey, boy! You know the butcher's shop at the corner? H-have they sold the prize turkey that was in the window?"

"What, the one as big as me? No sir."

"Well, go and buy it and take it round to Bob Cratchit's house in a Hackney cab. But mind you don't say who sent it! If you hurry, I'll give you half-a-crown!"

Then he dressed himself all in his best, and walked through the streets calling out, "Merry Christmas, everybody!" And every time he saw someone who owed him money, he said, "Don't worry about that twenty pounds. I don't need the money. Forget all about it. Oh, and Merry Christmas!"

He went to his nephew's house and invited himself to dinner — and had the merriest, most wonderful Christmas he had ever had in his life!

But he was at the office early next day. He wanted to get there before Bob Cratchit. And he did. Bob was two minutes late.

"What do you mean by coming in here at this time of day?" growled Scrooge.

"I'm very sorry, sir," said Bob, in terror of losing his job. "I had such a wonderful Christmas yesterday . . . such an amazing thing happened. But I promise this won't happen again, Mr Scrooge, sir."

"I can promise you it won't!" said Scrooge. "I'm not going to stand for this sort of thing any longer. So . . ." He stood up and gave Bob such a dig in the ribs that the clerk almost fell over. "So . . . I'm about to raise your wages and shorten your hours! Merry Christmas, Bob! Stoke up the fire, and then come into my office. I want you to tell me how I can help that splendid family of yours."

So Tiny Tim did not die, and no more ghosts visited Scrooge in the middle of the night. In fact, ever afterwards it was said of him that he knew how to celebrate Christmas better than any man alive.

And so, as Tiny Tim observed when he saw the turkey arrive by Hackney cab that Christmas morning,

"God bless us, every one!"

We Wish You A Merry Christmas

We wish you a merry Christmas,
We wish you a merry Christmas,
We wish you a merry Christmas,
And a happy New Year.

Good tidings we bring to you and your kin.
We wish you a merry Christmas
And a happy New Year.

We all want some figgy pudding,
We all want some figgy pudding,
We all want some figgy pudding,
So bring some out here!

We won't go until we get some,
We won't go until we get some,
We won't go until we get some,
So bring some out here!

We wish you a merry Christmas,
We wish you a merry Christmas,
We wish you a merry Christmas,
And a happy New Year.

BOO HO HO!

It was on Christmas Eve, of all the days of the year, that Rudolph found Santa crying.

"I'm sorry. It's silly of me," said Santa. "Pretend you didn't see." And he blew his nose with a giant handkerchief.

"Ah, you've been overdoing it," said Rudolph gently. "Next week you must put your feet up and have a good rest."

"Yes, yes. I expect that's it." Santa sniffed and tried to put on a brave smile. "Ho ho ho . . ." he tried to chuckle, but it soon slithered into a "boo hoo hoo" and he rested his head on his arms and cried. "Oh Rudolph! I know I am a silly, selfish old man, but if only I could see it just once . . . just *once!*"

"See what? What's the matter? You can tell me. See what?"

"*Christmas,* of course!" Santa shook his head and attempted another laugh. But it was no good. "Ho ho ho, boo hoo! All night long on Christmas Eve, creeping about on slippery roofs, being careful not to wake babies, always trying to remember what children have asked for. I suppose they like what I take them. I mean, they go on asking for things, year in, year out. I hear rumours that people enjoy Christmas. But how would I know? I come straight back here, have a large turkey sandwich with you and the other reindeer, and then fall into bed totally exhausted."

stairs. If we dress up as skiers or clowns — angels even — we can visit lots of families, play with the children, and join in all the fun."

So that night, after Santa had made his Christmas deliveries, he changed his usual route. Instead of turning towards the North Pole and home, he parked the sleigh in a little back street beside the park. While all the other reindeer had an early Christmas dinner of some delicious leaves, Rudolph and Santa changed their clothes in the bushes.

Early next morning they wandered through the snowy streets wearing bobble hats and goggles, with skis slung over their shoulders. People were just beginning to stir. From behind upstairs windows came the rustle of wrapping paper and squeals of delight as children opened their presents. "Look! Look what I've got!" "That's fantastic!" "Can I play with it now?"

Rudolph glanced sideways at Santa and saw him grinning.

"They *do* seem pleased," said Santa, smiling shyly.

Rudolph stood in front of Santa's fire thinking, and the snow on his thick coat dripped meltingly into the rug. "It won't be the same *this* year, Santa," he said at last. "You'll have a *proper* Christmas this year, you wait and see. What we need is a couple of good disguises. There are lots of old clothes in your cupboard under the

When they knocked at number 14, and Mrs Smith opened the door, they could see past her to where her six daughters were opening presents around the Christmas tree. They all looked so happy with the gifts Santa had delivered the night before that his ski goggles became quite misty with pleasure as he watched them with their toys.

"Hello!" said Santa warmly. "We were just passing and we thought we would knock on your door and wish you all 'A Happy Christmas'. You can ask us in if you like."

"I don't know you. It's Christmas and anyway I'm far too busy. Come back next week." And she shut the door with a bang.

"Oh dear," said Rudolph, disappointed. They went back to the park and changed into their clown costumes and knocked at another door in the street.

"I've got the dinner to cook," said Mrs Jones at number 32. "What do you want?" Behind her, her four sons were playing with an electric train set. This had been the most difficult present of all for Santa to fit down a chimney. But it seemed worthwhile, now that he could see just how much pleasure the electric train set gave them.

"We thought you and your family might enjoy a few jokes, tricks, stories," Rudolph was saying. "So if you'd just invite us in . . ."

"Strangers? At Christmas? Christmas is a family time. Sorry." And Mrs Jones slammed the door sharply, with the most tremendous bang.

Rudolph glanced at Santa and saw his lip was trembling. They changed into their angel costumes and sang carols outside number 48 where children were playing the whistles Santa had delivered the night before.

"Clear off, or I'll set the dogs on you!" shouted Mr Brown from the bedroom window. "Isn't it bad enough to have the kids playing those wretched whistles without listening to you?"

Santa hitched up his angel's skirts and ran all the way back to the sleigh. Rudolph could hardly keep up. They galloped to the North Pole, without a word spoken between them.

What Wanda Wanted

On her way to bed one Christmas Eve, Wanda said: "I want a gold and silver dress, and I want lots of pretty jewels and I want long golden ringlets. I want it to be always Christmas, with people giving me things, and I want to know everything without ever going to school."

Her father sighed. "Your mother and I just can't afford all the things you want, Wanda." His daughter stamped her foot.

So that night Wanda set off on a journey across the world. She walked and walked until she passed a tall house. There was a glass coach with six white horses waiting in front of it. And beside the coach stood an elderly lady.

Down the steps came the prettiest girl Wanda had ever seen, wearing a beautiful dress of gold and silver lace.

At once Wanda said: "Oh how I want that dress."

The old lady looked from Wanda to the pretty girl and back again. Then she sighed and said: "Oh. Go indoors Cinderella. What Wanda wants, Wanda must have."

So the girl went back and took off the dress. Wanda put it on — it fitted perfectly.

At the edge of the city, lay the forest. A tangle of rose briars blocked her way. Someone was hacking through them, for the briars shook to the sound of chopping.

"Hello there!" called Wanda. The most handsome prince she had ever seen emerged and leaned on his sword to catch his breath. The sword's hilt shone with every kind of precious gem. "Good evening, maiden. I don't know how long it will take me to cut through these roses to rescue Sleeping Beauty. You had better go another way."

Wanda was not listening. "Oh! If only I could have the beautiful jewels in your sword!"

The prince turned a little pale, and

his smile faltered. "What Wanda wants, Wanda must have." He bowed low, presented her with his sword, then mounted his horse and rode away.

With the jewelled sword through her sash, Wanda danced off across the desert to where the sea pounded on a rocky shore. There, in the window of a high tower, sat Rapunzel, the happiest woman Wanda had ever seen. Her golden hair trickled down the wall, twining amongst trembling passion flowers. She whispered to Wanda: "I hope you are as happy as I am, little girl."

"I would be if I had hair like yours," said Wanda, her voice sour with jealousy. Rapunzel's smile melted away. "What Wanda wants, Wanda must have."

She withdrew from the window and returned with a pair of gold scissors. "Take whatever you want." So Wanda climbed and snipped, climbed and snipped — every last ringlet of hair. She fastened it to her own with tendrils of passion flowers, and went on her way.

On top of the world, she came to a dreadful place where the cog-wheel stands which turns the Earth. And there, straining with all his might to hold the wheel still, stood the Man-Who-Knows.

"Ooh it's so cold here," said Wanda.

"Wanda wants it to be always Christmas," explained the Man. "So *this* side of the world must always be winter."

Wanda wasn't listening. "I want to know everything, without having to go to school."

"Mmm, I'll tell you just four things," he said. "Far away, in a big town, Cinderella is crying. Wanda wanted her dress so now Cinderella cannot go to the ball.

"Deep in the forest, Sleeping Beauty lies spellbound for ever. The prince who should have woken her has no sword to cut through the briars.

"High in a tower, Rapunzel sits crying. Her prince came back to marry her. But he did not know his love without her golden hair, so he rode away for ever."

"Stop! Stop!" cried Wanda. "Is everyone in the world unhappy because of me?" And she covered her ears in shame.

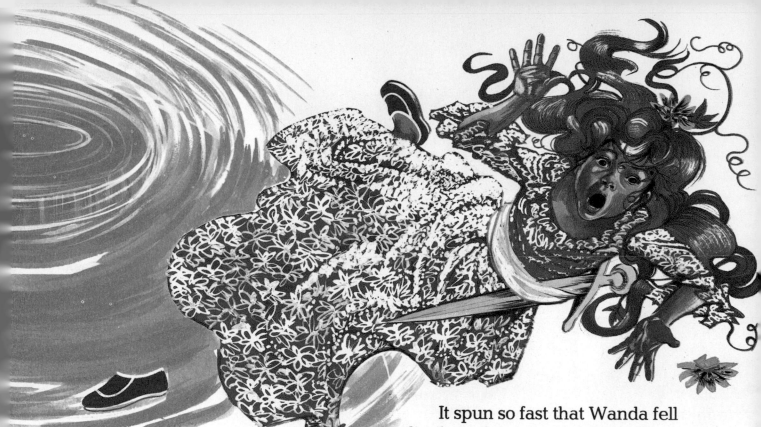

It spun so fast that Wanda fell dizzily to the ground. When she came to, she was lying in bed at home — just as she had been on Christmas Eve. "Mother! *Mother!*" she called. "What day is it? I want to know what day it is . . ."

"Why, it's Christmas morning," said her mother.

"Oh thank goodness," said Wanda. "I think I must have been dreaming. I do so want to give you and Daddy these presents so that we can have a happy Christmas together."

"Oh no, my dear. I know for a fact that your mother and father are glad you went away. Even now they're saying: 'What a mercy not to have to keep buying Wanda what she wants.'"

"I don't want to know. I don't want it to be true! I don't want any of it to have happened!"

"Well! To make that so," said the Man-Who-Knows, "I'd have to turn the world back to yesterday. I've never done that before."

"Oh turn it!" begged Wanda. "Let me help. Oh I do so WANT to undo today!"

"What Wanda wants, Wanda must have," laughed the Man. And with one gigantic push they rolled the world back one whole day.

The Great Sleigh Robbery

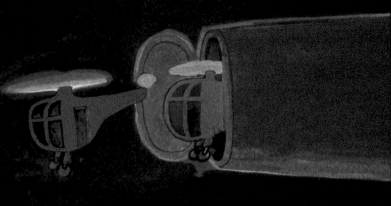

On top of the tallest building in the city, the most successful robbers in the world planned their greatest robbery. Santa Claus was to be their victim.

They had a clever plan in which their disguise expert had made exact copies of Santa's costume so that no-one would be able to tell Santa and the robbers apart.

Just before Christmas Eve the robbers were ready. They boarded a special

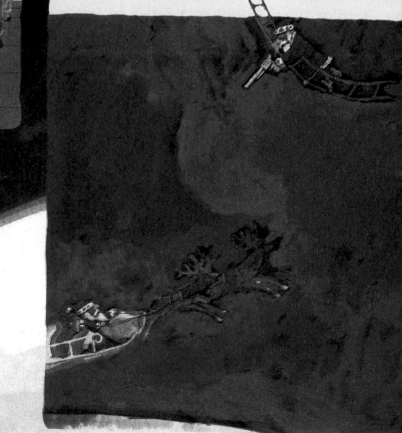

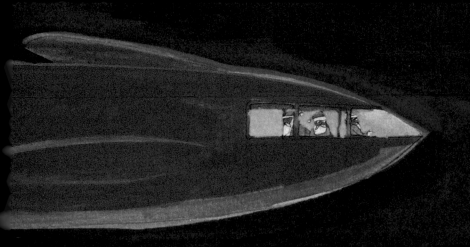

rocket and headed for their destination.

At last they heard the sound of sleigh-bells. Swiftly, twenty-four robbers climbed into twelve helicopters. Doors opened at the back of the rocket and out they flew.

Swooping down, they surrounded Santa Claus and pointed pistols at him.

"Do as you're told, Santa," said one robber, "and you won't be hurt."

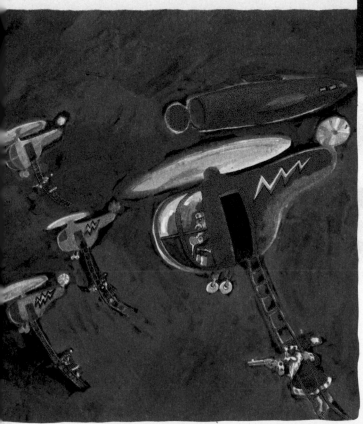

They forced Santa to drive his sleigh inside the rocket and the helicopters followed. The doors closed and the rocket soared high into the sky.

But the robbers had made one mistake. They had forgotten that at Christmas time children lie awake, listening for sleigh-bells and watching for a glimpse of Santa Claus. And so millions of children *saw* what happened. Dressing quickly, they all ran from their homes.

Quick as a flash, word of the kidnapping spread all over the world.

The robbers flew high and south over the sea until they were near their hide-out. They tried to land, but just before the rocket touched down, hundreds of children ran from the bushes, shouting angrily. The rocket climbed up into the sky again and flew farther away over another sea.

Now the robbers looked down on a wide flat desert. But here, too, crowds of angry children were arriving.

Again the rocket could not land.

Next the rocket flew over dark jungles. The trees were so close together that there was no room for the rocket to land, but even so the jungle was full of children.

The robbers tried flying east.

They flew high over mountains.

And low over wide plains and rice fields.

They flew high above the Pacific Ocean, over big cities, farmlands, and tall pine forests.

But wherever they went they saw below them angry children pointing to the sky.

Even the vast ice-fields of the North Pole were alive with their cries.

"This is hopeless," moaned the robber pilot, "we'll have to give up.

There's nowhere for us to land."

"Yeah," said another robber, untying Santa Claus, "but we'll have our revenge, Mr Claus. There'll be another chance next year."

"All I fear at the moment," said Santa Claus, "is disappointing the children. You have made me late delivering their presents. Now you must help me make up for lost time."

The robbers realised that they had no choice, and so they agreed to help. Back they flew, over the North Pole, the cities, deserts, jungles, oceans and mountains, still with angry shouts ringing in their ears.

But all along the way Santa stopped the rocket, the helicopters flew out, and the robbers, laden with presents, slid down chimneys.

Then a surprising thing happened.

The children's angry shouts turned to cheers! The robbers were amazed, and they began to enjoy themselves. This was far more fun than stealing!

At last the work was finished. The robbers were tired and Santa's cups of tea were very welcome. "Can we help you again, Mr Claus?" said one. "We've had such a good time."

Three of the toughest robbers groaned. Once was enough for them! Stuffing their pockets with Santa's best silver teaspoons, they rushed off through the snow.

The remaining robbers finished their tea. "Can't we help you make the toys for next year?" they asked. "We've got lots of good ideas."

In fact, the robbers are still working for Santa Claus.

They are very good at inventing new toys. They have probably made some of your favourites. The robbers are happy and have no wish to leave and never go on strike, because they are surrounded by gifts and tinsel and bright wrapping paper, so every day is like Christmas Day to the Great Sleigh Robbers.

DING DONG MERRILY ON HIGH!

Ding dong! Merrily on high
In heaven the bells are ringing.
Ding dong! Verily the sky
Is riven with angel singing.
(Ding dong! . . . Ding dong!)
Gloria, Hosanna in excelsis!

E'en so there below, below,
Let steeple bells be swungen.
And i-o, i-o, i-o,
By priest and people sungen.
(Ding dong! . . . Ding dong!)
Gloria, Hosanna in excelsis!

Pray you, dutifully prime
Your matin chime, ye ringers:
May you beautifully rhyme
Your evening song, ye singers.
(Ding dong! . . . Ding dong!)
Gloria, Hosanna in excelsis!

Silent Night

Silent night, holy night,
All is calm, all is bright.
'Round yon virgin mother and child,
Holy infant so tender and mild,
Sleep in heavenly peace,
Sleep in heavenly peace.

Silent night, holy night,
Shepherds quake at the sight;
Glories stream from heaven afar,
Heavenly hosts sing Alleluia!
Christ the saviour is born!
Christ the saviour is born!

Silent night, holy night,
Son of God, love's pure light;
Radiance beams from thy holy face,
With the dawn of redeeming grace,
Jesus, Lord, at thy birth,
Jesus, Lord, at thy birth.